Best Wishes to Marty
from Paul Goble.

Denver 1987.

STAR BOY

BRADBURY PRESS • SCARSDALE, NEW YORK

STAR BOY

Retold and Illustrated by PAUL GOBLE

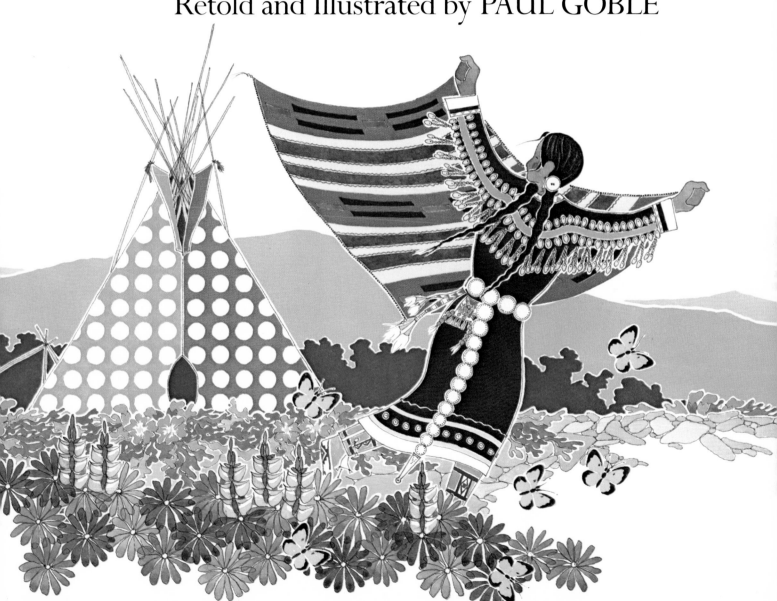

This is the ancient story of how the sacred knowledge of the Sun Dance was given to the Blackfeet. It is retold here, with respect, in its narrative form for children. The full story, published in several versions, is best found in The Old North Trail by Walter McClintock (1910) and Blackfoot Lodge Tales by George Bird Grinnell (1892).

The Blackfeet were nomadic hunters who traveled over a wide area of the northern plains. They now live on the western edge of their former lands, close to the Rocky Mountains in Montana, USA and Alberta, Canada. As in the old days, the tribes gather each summer and pitch their painted tipis for the Sun Dance.

Text and illustrations copyright © 1983 by Paul Goble. All rights reserved. No part of this book may be reproduced in any form or by any means, except for the inclusion of brief quotations in a review, without permission in writing from the publisher. Manufactured in the United States of America.   3 2 1 83 84 85.   The text of this book is set in 18 pt. Perpetua. The illustrations are India ink and watercolor, reproduced in combined line and halftone.
Library of Congress Cataloging in Publication Data
Goble, Paul. Star boy.
Summary: Relates the Blackfoot Indian legend in which Star Boy gains the Sun's forgiveness for his mother's disobedience and is allowed to return to the Sky World.
1. Siksika Indians — Legends.   2. Indians of North America — West (U.S.) — Legends. [1. Siksika Indians — Legends. 2. Indians of North America — Legends]
I. Title.
E99.S54G62 1983   398.2′08997   [392.2]   [E]   82-20599   ISBN 0-02-722660-3

for Janet and Robert

One summer evening two sisters took their blankets outside and fell asleep.

They awoke as day was breaking and the Morning Star was shining brightly.

"I love Morning Star," said the older sister. "He is the only star who knows both night and day. He is so handsome. Morning Star is my husband."

Later the girl went to the river for water. A young man stood in her path.

"Please let me pass," she said modestly, "I do not know you."

"But I am your husband, Morning Star," the young man answered.

And then she saw who stood before her; he was straight and handsome like no other man.

"Come," he said, holding above her a juniper branch in which a spider had woven its web. "We shall go to my home in the Sky World. Close your eyes." He wrapped his painted robe around them, and spoke to the spider. As he did, they were lifted up into the sky.

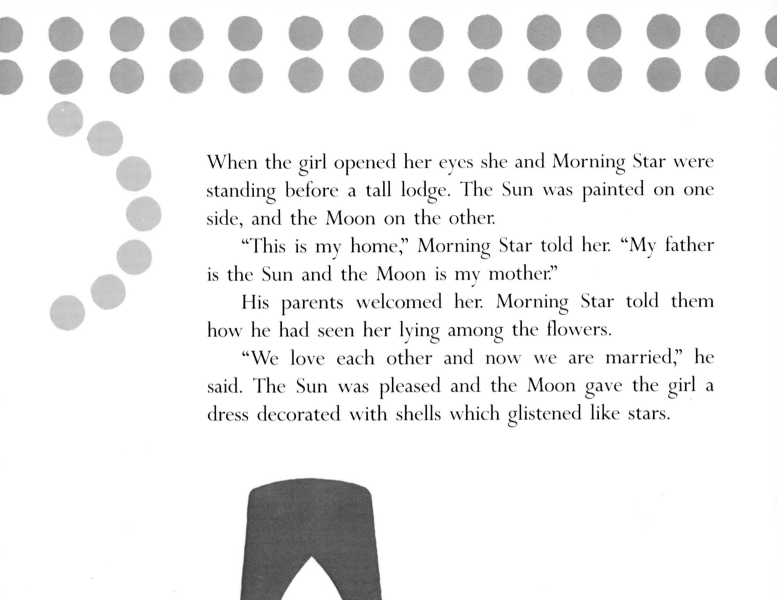

When the girl opened her eyes she and Morning Star were standing before a tall lodge. The Sun was painted on one side, and the Moon on the other.

"This is my home," Morning Star told her. "My father is the Sun and the Moon is my mother."

His parents welcomed her. Morning Star told them how he had seen her lying among the flowers.

"We love each other and now we are married," he said. The Sun was pleased and the Moon gave the girl a dress decorated with shells which glistened like stars.

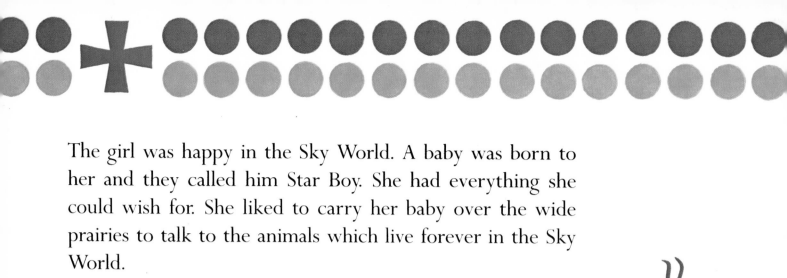

The girl was happy in the Sky World. A baby was born to her and they called him Star Boy. She had everything she could wish for. She liked to carry her baby over the wide prairies to talk to the animals which live forever in the Sky World.

One day the Moon gave the girl a stick to dig up roots.

"Dig up any plants you wish," she said, "but do not dig the plants with the pink flowers. If you dig up any of these roots it will bring great unhappiness to us all."

The girl often used to wonder about the Moon's warning. She was curious about the plants with the pink flowers. Surely it would not matter to dig up just one root, she decided. She dug around the plant, but when she pulled out the root it left a hole through the Sky World. Looking down she saw her old home far below. Everyone down there looked so happy and busy. She could see her mother and father and her younger sister and she was sad she could not be with them. Suddenly she felt very lonely.

The Moon saw she had been crying.

"Oh my daughter, you have dug up the root I told you not to dig."

The Sun was angry and also sad at her disobedience, "Now your heart will always be in two places; you will never be happy here, nor in the world below. You must go back to your people."

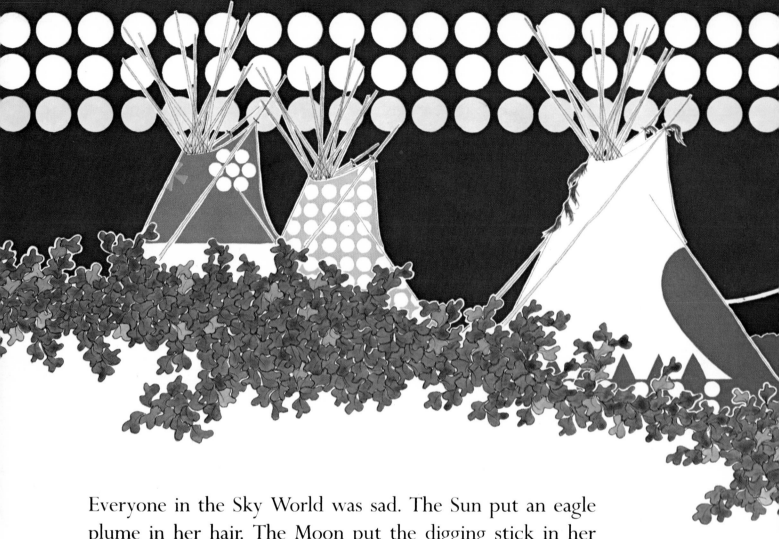

Everyone in the Sky World was sad. The Sun put an eagle plume in her hair. The Moon put the digging stick in her hand. She held Star Boy in her arms, and Morning Star wrapped his wife and baby in his painted robe. He let them down through the hole with the spider's web.

On earth the people saw a bright star falling and ran to where it landed. There they found the girl and Star Boy asleep on Morning Star's own robe.

The girl was never happy after that. It was not until she died that she was taken back again to the Sky World. She became the Evening Star and lives there with Morning Star forever.

Star Boy was still young when his mother died. As he grew, people noticed his face became more and more ugly with a mysterious scar. People said the Sun had put it there because of his mother's disobedience in the Sky World. Everyone feared the awful scar. They called him Scarface.

When Star Boy grew up he loved the chief's beautiful daughter, but he did not tell her because he was poor and ugly. Many young men wanted to marry her.

But when he saw that she rejected them, he found courage to speak to her: "I am poor and have no fine clothes, but you are always in my heart. Will you marry me?"

"I have waited for you to ask me," she answered, "but the Sun has told me that I cannot marry without his blessing. Go back to the Sky World where you were born; tell your grandfather that what is in your heart is also in mine. As a sign of his blessing, ask him to take away the scar from your face."

Star Boy felt full of hope, yet also despair: "How will I ever find the way to the Sky World?"

"Take courage! Try hard!" she said. "You will find the way!"

Not even the wise men could tell Star Boy the way to the Sky World, and so he asked the birds and animals because they have a different kind of wisdom.

They all told him: "Go to the place where the Sun sinks down each evening; there you will find his lodge."

He climbed over the mountains and through the forests listening to the whispering aspens and pine trees. Joyful flocks of cranes flying like floating ribbons high in the sky encouraged him to go on. The elk called out to him: "Go to the place where the Sun sinks down each evening; there you will find his lodge."

One day, tired with walking so far, Star Boy came to the end of the land. Before him spread a great water. His journey seemed to end at the water's edge.

As night began to fall two loons appeared swimming from the shore. Suddenly Star Boy was not tired any more. He rose and followed the shining path the loons left behind them. The path led him up into the Sky World.

There, at last, he found the Sun's lodge.

When the Sun appeared Star Boy spoke to him: "Grandfather, I have traveled far to speak to you. I am your grandson, born here in the Sky World, but on earth I am the poorest of men. I have come to ask for your blessing. I love the beautiful daughter of the chief. We wish to marry, but I am ugly with the scar you once gave me in anger. Oh Grandfather, have pity on me. Give us your blessing so that we can marry; take away the scar."

His Grandfather lifted up his face and looked at Star Boy.

"I give you the one you love," he said. "I know she has been wise; a pure woman shall live a long time and so shall her family. Tell your people," he said, "if they build a lodge in my honor each summer, I will restore their sick people to health." Then in the Sun's dazzling light, Star Boy felt the scar slowly fading away.

In a little while the Sun left on his journey across the sky.

Star Boy returned to earth down the rainbow.

People marveled when they saw the young man return. They remembered his face, but now his expression was radiant and the awful scar was gone. He was no longer poor but had fine clothes.

There was great rejoicing when their handsome Star Boy and his beautiful bride were married.

When Star Boy died he was taken back up into the Sky World. Low over the eastern horizon, before the Sun rises, Star Boy can sometimes be seen traveling together with his father, Morning Star. Star Boy can also sometimes be seen at nightfall walking with his mother, Evening Star. When the people see them they are glad to remember they have relatives in the Sky World.

During the summer, when the Sun reaches his highest place in the sky, they build a special lodge in his honor. The Sun Dance lodge is round like the earth and sky. It is supported by the sacred tree standing at the center, and, like the tipis, opens to the rising sun. Inside, the people dance and give thanks, and pray that the Creator will take away their scars and make their hearts new again, just as Star Boy was made new a long time ago.

We give thanks for the Sun who rises each day
to give warmth to the earth and also to the
hearts of men.
(Edgar Red Cloud)

SONG OF THE RISING SUN

With visible face I am appearing.
In a sacred manner I appear.
For the greening earth a pleasantness I make.
The center of the nation's hoop, I have made pleasant.
With visible face, behold me!
The four-leggeds and two-leggeds, I have made them to walk;
The wings of the air, I have made them to fly;
The finned ones, I have made them to swim;
The rooted ones, I have made them to rise.
With visible face I appear.
My day, I have made it holy.
(Black Elk)